This book belongs to

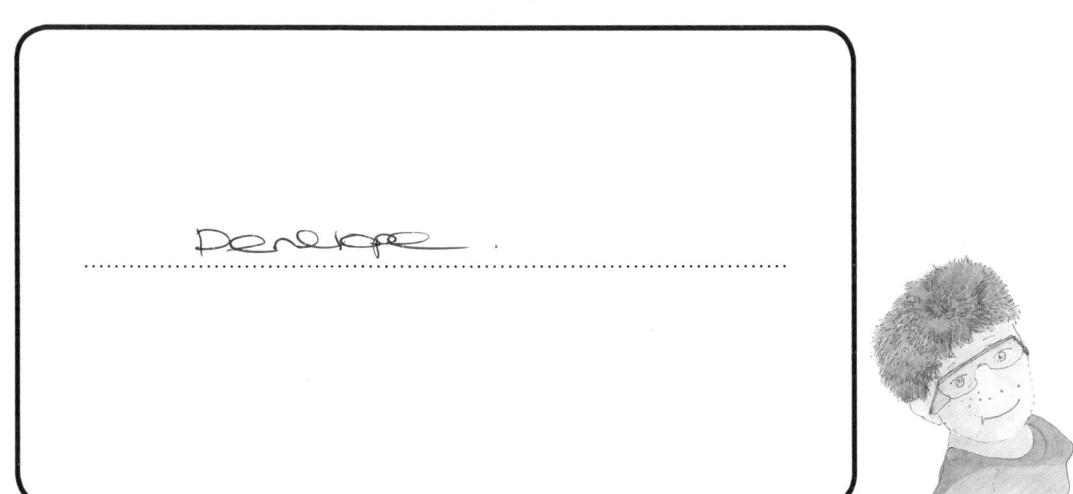

.... Penelope . ...

"We're the **Supersiblings** and our power is to **care**,

To make all things **inclusive** and teach the world to share.

We're the **Supersiblings** and our power knows no end,

If we don't know what to do, we simply **ask our friends**."

Let's meet the gang!

The Supersiblings Gang...

...all have one thing in common; their **brothers** and **sisters** all have **additional needs**. This has given them **special powers**, like exceptional knowledge on **disabilities**, an abundance of **empathy** and the **super** special ability of making sure everyone is always **included**!

The **Supersiblings Gang** meet every week and go on incredible adventures, to help their **brothers** and **sisters**. They travel far and wide, to teach their friends how to help and interact with **children** with **disabilities**.

Join this **incredible** gang of **super boys** and **super girls**, who are working hard to make sure that no child is ever **excluded** and if you're lucky, you might even learn their **Supersibling** chant along the way!

Foreword

As a psychotherapist working with both adults and children for over 15 years, I understand the importance of feeling included for a person's sense of who they are in the world – for self-esteem, confidence and mental well-being.

This book gives children, their families and their friends' insight into what it's like to feel excluded and captures the positive power of talking, of working together, of enquiring. It is both thought provoking and empowering – both for those feeling excluded and for those around them who may simply not notice or not understand how to include them.

Adelle's story conveys a vital and simple message in a fun way – if you don't know how to include someone who may be different, just ask them.

Jo Frost
MSc (Psych), PG Dip, UKCP reg.
MBACP Psychotherapist
jofrostpsychotherapy.com

Written by Adelle Spindlove
Illustrations by Claire S Bicknell

Freddie and the
High Flying Kick

For my 3 favourite boys & my Mama – AS

For Benjamin, Abigail, Raffi & Sebastian – Hold that Dream – CSB

Copyright © Adelle Spindlove 2021
Illustrations Copyright © Claire S Bicknell 2021

The rights of Adelle Spindlove and Claire S Bicknell to be identified as
the Author and Illustrator of the work has been asserted by them
in accordance with the Copyright, Designs and Patents Act 1988
Layout by White Magic Studios (www.whitemagicstudios.co.uk)

ISBN 978-1-8383681-0-4
Published by Rat & Tea Publishing 2021

High up in the treetops, a little gang does meet,
For lots of conversation and something sweet to eat.

There's Theo, Pam and Susie and little Ruben too.
Matilda, Luke and Leesa and Frankie, who is new.

They're called the Supersiblings
and they have a special power.
But once a week they sit
and take a break for just an hour,

To talk about their super work
and siblings in their care.
And this week at the meeting,
it's Frankie's turn to share.

8

"I don't know how to start."
Frankie said quite meek and mild.
"My brother's being picked on,
by another child.

He has a frame to help him walk
and they won't let him play.

No group games at break time,
it happens every day."

The gang all paused and shook their heads,
they'd heard it all before,
Then one by one they all stood up
and walked towards the door.

"We must go to the school and help" said Leesa nice and loud.
"It's time to see what we can do, to make our siblings proud."

They clambered down the ladder and then stood brave and tall,
Arms crossed high, side by side, a Superhero wall.

They whizzed off
to the playground,
like flying
birds
in V,

And saw a boy,
playing all alone,
a nasty sight to see.

11

"We're the Supersiblings!" said Luke as they arrived.
    "And there has been injustice!" Young Matilda cried.

The girls and boys all stopped their play,
        balls came tumbling down.
            The children stood and stared at them,
                their faces in a frown.

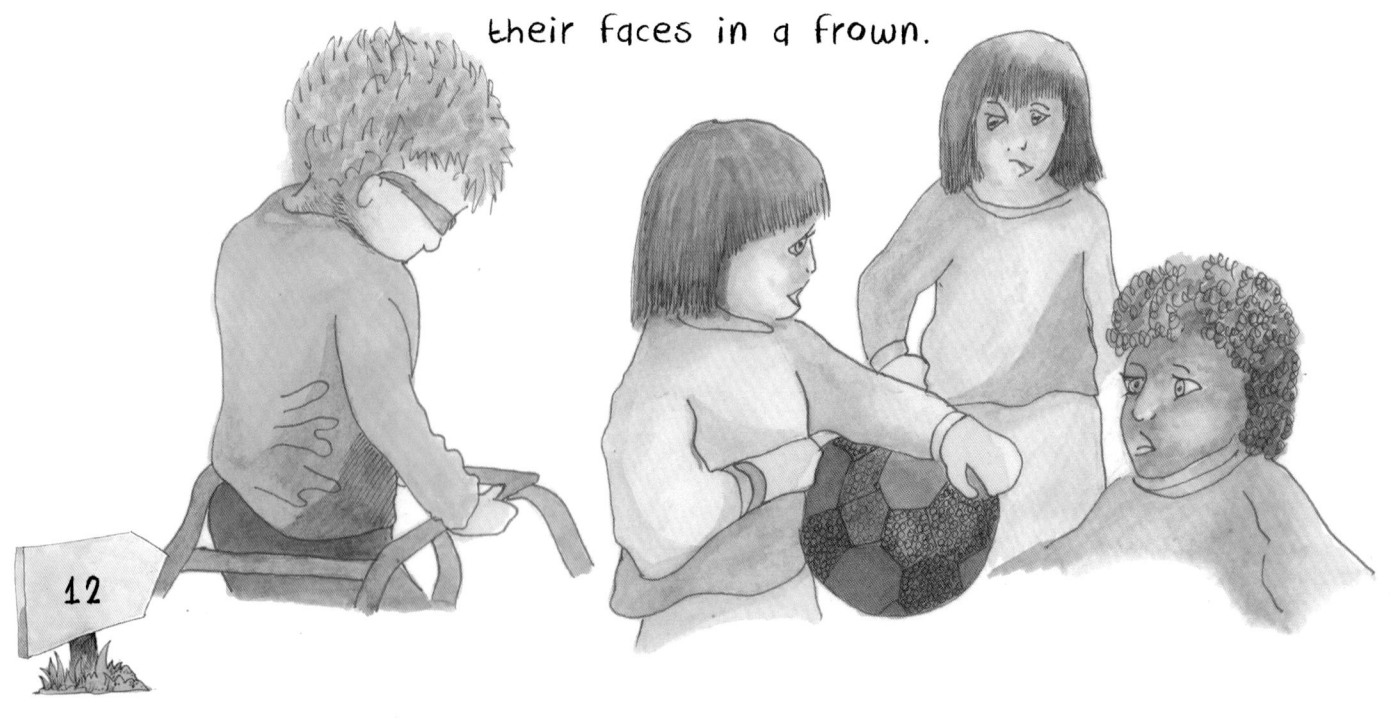

"We hear that there's been bullying"
said Ruben with a sigh.
The girls and boys all shook their heads,
some trying not to cry.

"I'm not a bully,"
said a girl,
dressed head
to toe in blue.

"We always play together,
I promise you it's true!"

The children all went silent,
eyes darting to their friends.
Nobody moved, nobody spoke,
unsure of how this ends.

"Everyone plays together?
No-one is left out?"
said Frankie holding back
the tears, voice rising to a shout.

They looked around the playground
and suddenly they saw,
A boy left out, all alone,
eyes staring at the floor.

"We're sorry" said the children, "but he is in that frame.
We don't know what to do, we can't change the game."

The Supersiblings all stood tall, preparing for their chant:
Of a world that's full of kindness,
where there's no such word as "can't".

They joined their hands together, hope shining from their eyes,
The children watched them sing, as their voices reached the skies.

"We're the Supersiblings and our power is to care,
To make all things inclusive and teach the world to share.

We're the Supersiblings
and our power knows no end,
If we don't know what to do,
we simply ask our friends."

16

"It's time for you to speak now" said Frankie to his bro,

"We can make them understand and teach them what we know."

"I am Fred" he whispered "but my family call me Freddie,

I'm really good at ball games, I can show you if you're ready?"

17

The boys and girls looked nervous as they nodded and agreed,
Then one boy stood and said to Fred
"Please tell me what you need?"

"I need someone to hold my hand and place the ball right here."
Freddie spoke, nice and loud, his voice showing no fear.

The children did as they were asked and then stood back to see,
The ball flying up, through the air, Fred's cheering filled with glee.

They all stood in amazement and then began to clap,
Fred's excitement growing, his arms moving with a flap.

19

The Supersiblings then watched on, their eyes full of delight,
As more balls were found and placed for Fred
to kick with all his might.

20

And so the supersiblings left,
their work today all done.

Freddie playing
with his friends,
included in the fun.

They rushed back to the treetops for another chance to share,
About their super lives and special siblings in their care.

For they're the Supersiblings and their power knows no end
And when they don't know what to do,
they simply ASK THEIR FRIENDS!

Thank you so much for reading this book.
We hope you enjoyed learning all about the Supersiblings Gang,
especially Frankie and his brother Freddie!

Want to join the gang?

We are looking for more people to join the Supersiblings and we think that you are exactly the right person to join the gang, but just to be sure, we have a few questions:

Do you....

...ask other children to play, not just your friends?

☐

...make sure that nobody is sitting alone at lunchtime,
or in the playground?

☐

...talk to children who have different interests to you?

☐

...ask questions to discover more about your friends?

☐

...ask for help, if you're not sure what to do?

☐

If you ticked yes to the questions above, then welcome to the gang. We are so happy to have you with us!

If you didn't, please don't worry, but the next time you go to school, or the park, you can try some of the things above.

If you would like to know more about the gang, or would like to tell us about your own Super Adventures, then please contact Adelle, the writer of the book.

Acknowledgements

This book would not have been possible without the generosity, support and belief of the following people:

Abby & Matt Croucher
Abi & Marcus Bailey
Adam Taussik
Alan & Maureen Harding
Alex Horton
Alfred & Judy Buerling
Alistair Walker
Amanda Bowles
Ann Griffiths
Arnold van Os
Ashleigh Kerr-Habets
Barbara Barret
Christine McCann
Claire Jones
Claire Newton
Clare Munro
David & Shirley Kett
Dawn Harris
Deborah Goldberg
Duncan Findlay
Emily Bell
Emily Bryczkowski
Emily Garside
Emma & Paul Freeman
Emma Perfitt
Faye Figgins
Gemma & Luke Nuckley
Gemma Payne
Gina Hodsman
Greg Taussik
Heather Peattie
Helen Cusworth
Henry Thurstan

Jake & Sally Morries
Janet & Murray Boaz
Janet Meyer
Jane & Tom Taussik
Janet & Steve Morries
Jenny Paterson
Jill Desborough
Jill Long
Jo Hamilton
Jodi Gray
Jodie Gosney-Morries
Jody Matthews
John & Taryn Thomson
John Taussik
Jon & Nicola Woods
Josette van Os
Josh & Leesa Turner
Julie Weber
Jung-A Bourner
Katherine Taylor
Katy Beckett
Kelly Winn
Laura Ambrose
Lily Tucker
Louise Lee
Lucile & Andy Sturges
Luke & Laura Spindlove
Lydia & Simon Wade
Marilyn Lunn
Mark Rumens
Michael Bone
Mike & Alison Freeman
Natalie Brett

Nichola & Rob Derry
Nichola & Leslie Ho
Pat Gray
Pat Huxtable
Paula McGaughey
Pauline Nixon
Prue Amner
Rachel & Thomas Deering
Rebecca Altman
Ronnie Livia
Rosina Figgins
Ruth & Matt Johnson
Sam Bone
Sandy Scott
Sara Boilen
Sara Thelwell
Sarah Pearson
Sharon McDermott
Shereen Toorabally
Sian Macleod
Simon & Rikki Bone
Stella Parkin
Sue Spindlove
Sue Taylor
Suzette Taplin
Tom Allison
Tracy Ewell
Vanessa Davies
Vicky Halliday
Wendy Austin-Ward
Will and Kirsty Dixon

Thank you so much for believing in this project!  25

Special Thanks...

...to the following businesses, who have been incredible in raising awareness, donating and providing support.

ABC Concerts: www.abcconcerts.com

Baby Sensory: www.babysensory.com

Boogie Mites, Hayling Island: www.boogiemites.co.uk

English Sara, Southampton: www.englishsara.co.uk

Hive Portsmouth: www.hiveportsmouth.org.uk

Sanctuary Home Healing: www.sanctuaryhomehealing.co.uk

Sing and Sign, Portsmouth: www.singandsign.co.uk

Waterbabies, Portsmouth: www.waterbabies.co.uk

Babies go Bananas, Portsmouth: FB @babiesgobananasplaygroup

Rainbow Bubbles Sensory, Portsmouth: FB @rainbowbubbles

PSKO is an established Martial Arts Organisation with 35+ years' experience located in Havant on the South coast of England. They offer beginner classes up to competitive training.

www.psko-karate.com

Please contact PSKO for the opportunity to train with:

Michael Fletcher, Sensei 5th dan   Chief Instructor and Examiner

Samantha Lewington, Sensei 2nd dan   Assistant Chief Instructor

Alan Jackson, Sensei 1st dan   Instructor

Organisations for Support and Advice

Contact: www.contact.org.uk

Kids: www.kids.org.uk

Scope: www.scope.org.uk

Sibs: www.sibs.org.uk

Siblings: www.skybadger.co.uk

BECAUSE OF YOU, SIB
EMPOWERING SIBS TO THRIVE

Because of You, Sib is a company where you can find life coaching, community, mental wellness, self-love strategies & digital resources for navigating life as "the other sibling."

For more information please visit www.becauseofyousib.com
Or follow on Instagram @becauseofyousib

Super Siblings is a safe space for children to socialise with others who understand their situation. Their support group sessions are welcoming and fun and have been designed to relieve children of any mental and emotional strain, they may be experiencing.

For more information please visit www.supersiblings.org

About Us

Adelle Spindlove – Writer

Adelle lives in Portsmouth with her partner and their two children. Her eldest son has a rare neuro-developmental syndrome called ADNP, while the youngest son is neuro-typical, her very own super sibling. When she is not writing, she enjoys swimming in the sea, dancing in the kitchen and of course reading lots and lots of books to her boys.

This is her first book for children and she hopes you enjoy reading it, as much as she enjoyed writing it.

If you would like to know more or wish to contact the writer, then please visit www.adellespindlove.com

Claire S Bicknell – Illustrator

Claire lives in Wiltshire with her husband and four children, Benjamin, Abigail and twins Raffi & Sebastian. Claire designs and illustrates professionally and personally and is rarely far from her art board, fulfilling a lifelong dream she had aged 6 to draw for a living. Passions include her cats and Bernese Mountain dogs, illustrating endangered animals, cycling, baking and eating chocolate! Claire loves to create educational, imaginative rainbows of hope and colour on the pages for all children to enjoy and delight in – big and small.

If you would like to know more then please visit her linked in profile (claire-s-bicknell-marks) or Bark.com gallery: Claire S Bicknell. Or you can email her at claire@stylographics.com